DON'T MISS CATALINA'S OTHER MAGICAL ADVENTURES!

The New Friend Fix

Off-Key

BY JENNIFER TORRES

CATALINA INCOGNITO

ILLUSTRATED BY
GLADYS JOSE

ALADDIN
New York London Toronto Sydney New Delhi

ALADDIN
An imprint of Simon & Schuster Children's Publishing Division
1230 Avenue of the Americas, New York, New York 10020
First Aladdin paperback edition March 2022
Text copyright © 2022 by Jennifer Torres
Illustrations copyright © 2022 by Gladys Jose
Also available in an Aladdin hardcover edition.
All rights reserved, including the right of reproduction in whole or in part in any form.
ALADDIN and related logo are registered trademarks of Simon & Schuster, Inc.
For information about special discounts for bulk purchases, please contact
Simon & Schuster Special Sales at 1-866-506-1949 or business@simonandschuster.com.
The Simon & Schuster Speakers Bureau can bring authors to your live event. For more
information or to book an event contact the Simon & Schuster Speakers Bureau
at 1-866-248-3049 or visit our website at www.simonspeakers.com.
Book designed by Laura Lyn DiSiena
The illustrations for this book were rendered digitally.
The text of this book was set in Century Schoolbook.
Manufactured in the United States of America 0223 OFF
4 6 8 10 9 7 5 3
Library of Congress Cataloging-in-Publication Data
Names: Torres, Jennifer, 1980- author. | Jose, Gladys, illustrator.
Title: Catalina incognito / by Jennifer Torres ; illustrated by Gladys Jose.
Description: First Aladdin paperback edition. | New York : Aladdin, 2022. |
Series: Catalina incognito ; book 1 | Audience: Ages 6 to 9. | Summary: Eight-year-old
Catalina Castañeda uses Tía Abuela's sewing kit to turn ordinary clothing into a magical
disguise, enabling her to uncover a thief at the local library.
Identifiers: LCCN 2021005136 (print) | LCCN 2021005137 (ebook) |
ISBN 9781534482791 (hc) | ISBN 9781534482784 (pbk) | ISBN 9781534482807 (ebook)
Subjects: CYAC: Disguise—Fiction. | Stealing—Fiction. | Persistence—Fiction. |
Magic—Fiction. | Great aunts—Fiction. | Hispanic Americans—Fiction.
Classification: LCC PZ7.1.T65 Cat 2022 (print) | LCC PZ7.1.T65 (ebook) | DDC [Fic]—dc23
LC record available at https://lccn.loc.gov/2021005136
LC ebook record available at https://lccn.loc.gov/2021005137

FOR MY NANA, JOSEPHINE, WHO TAUGHT
ME THE MAGIC OF CREATIVITY

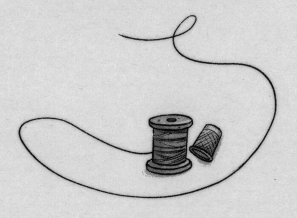

CONTENTS

CHAPTER 1   ATTENTION TO DETAIL   1

CHAPTER 2   YOU MIGHT BE SURPRISED   10

CHAPTER 3   SHOO   21

CHAPTER 4   THE BASICS   31

CHAPTER 5   THE BIG REVEAL   39

CHAPTER 6   INCOGNITO   50

CHAPTER 7   LONG-LOST TWIN   57

CHAPTER 8   BETTER THAN BEFORE   63

CHAPTER 9   ACCIDENTS HAPPEN   70

CHAPTER 10   SECRET MISSION   76

CHAPTER 11   CLUES   86

CHAPTER 12   LOST   95

CHAPTER 13   THE START   98

ACKNOWLEDGMENTS   105

CHAPTER 1

ATTENTION TO DETAIL

The picture on the puzzle box shows three gray kittens peeking out of a picnic basket.

Kittens. Of *course*.

If Mami and Papi didn't give me a kitten puzzle for my birthday, they would give me a kitten sticker collection. And if they didn't give me a kitten sticker collection, they would give me a kitten coloring book. Even though they know I am getting too old for all this kitten stuff. And even though I have told them to quit calling me "Kitty-Cat" and start using my real name, Catalina.

Everyone in my family—Mami and Papi; Baby Carlos in his high chair; my big sister, Coco; and Tía Abuela—is sitting around the kitchen table. They all lean forward, watching me.

"Well, Kitty-Cat," Papi asks, "what do you think?"

The first thing I think is, *Quit calling me "Kitty-Cat."*

But that's not what I say, because the *second* thing I think is that even though I don't love kittens as much as I used to, I still love puzzles. You get to figure out exactly where each piece belongs, and when you're finished, you know you haven't made any mistakes.

"It's perfect," I say.

"Maybe we can work on it together," Mami suggests.

Carlos claps. A droplet of drool drips off his lip and onto the high chair tray. I picture it landing on my puzzle. I fold my arms over the box to protect it from even the *idea* of Carlos's baby slobber.

"Hmm," I reply. Not quite a yes, and not exactly a no.

Luckily, Coco slides her gift across the table before I have to give a real answer.

She has wrapped it in this morning's newspaper. And lots and lots of tape. I don't have to open it to know what's inside—her old skateboard helmet.

"I'll even let you borrow my board," Coco says. She pulls the brim of her baseball cap lower down on her forehead. It hides her eyes, but not her smirk. "Unless you're still too scared after what happened the first time."

"I am *not* scared," I say, but my cheeks go warm as I remember last summer's wipeout.

Papi slaps his hands on the table. "Bravo, Coco!" he says. "Did you hear that, Kitty-Cat? Your sister is going to teach you to skateboard."

I don't need Coco to teach me, I think. This year I am ready. This year I will be perfect.

"Thank you, *Consuelo*," I say. I make my voice as sweet as a sip of horchata on a sunny afternoon. "You are *too* generous."

At last it is time to open Tía Abuela's gift. Tía Abuela's gifts are always the best.

Tía Abuela is Papi's aunt—my great-aunt—and her name is Catalina Castañeda too.

Only, most people know her as "La Chispa," the spark, one of the rottenest villains in telenovela history. Before she retired, the characters she played on TV were awfully, monstrously, fabulously *bad*. The rich but cruel stepmother. The beautiful but wicked duchess. The evil twin. Fans say her acting was so amazing, it was as if she *transformed* into every character.

Tía Abuela doesn't visit our house on the hill in Valle Grande very often. She's too busy traveling the world. But she always sends souvenirs home to my brother and sister and me.

Tía Abuela is only in town for the grand opening of the Catalina Castañeda Children's Room at the Valle Grande Central Library. The library was her favorite place to visit when she was growing up. It's where she first learned all about heroes and villains and adventures.

She's also here to celebrate my birthday, of course.

She has just returned from exploring the ancient Mayan city of Palenque in Mexico. Her gift comes in a box, wrapped in shimmering gold paper and a purple ribbon. I try to imagine what's inside. "An archaeologist's hand shovel?" I guess. "Ooh! I know, a map of the jungle!"

But when I untie the ribbon, tear apart the paper, and open the box, I don't find either of those things.

What I find instead is a red velvet pouch. It isn't new. Not even *almost* new. In fact, the pouch is so ancient, the cloth is worn bald in places.

It reminds me a little of an old dog with patchy fur. I try not to wrinkle my nose.

I know I should smile.

I know I should say "Thank you."

I know I should say *something*.

But I worry that if I so much as twitch, the groan I am trying to swallow will come tumbling out of my mouth before I can stop it.

"Not what you were expecting?" Tía Abuela says with a snort.

Not even close.

But it would be rude to just say so. So I don't.

I open the pouch and peer inside. There is a little brass thimble, a spool of silver thread, and a needle poking out of a strawberry-shaped pincushion.

Nope. Definitely not what I was expecting.

"Cata*lina* . . ." Mami nudges me with her voice. It's my name, but it is also a warning.

I try to think of something polite to say. "Thank you, Tía Abuela. It is so . . . so . . . so *different*."

Tía Abuela cackles. "Do you even know what it is, Kitty-Cat?"

I shake my head.

"It is a sewing kit. I've had it since I was your age. I thought it was the perfect gift for someone with your . . . How shall I put this?" She pauses. She taps a flamingo-pink fingernail against her lips as she thinks of the right thing to say. "Someone with your *attention to detail*. Attention to detail is very important when it comes to sewing."

"Hmm" is all I say.

CHAPTER 2

You Might Be Surprised

Carlos whines and squirms until Papi lifts him out of the high chair and plops him onto the floor. Then Carlos crawls toward the living room—and straight for Tía Abuela's giant purse.

"Not so fast, señor." Tía Abuela yanks the bag away just as Carlos is about to tip it upside down. She carries it upstairs, her long pink fingernails clicking on the handrail as she climbs.

In the kitchen Papi fills the sink with sudsy

water. Coco and I help Mami stack the dirty dishes until we hear a *rrrrrrroooooolllSMACK* on the sidewalk outside.

Our heads snap up. Skateboards.

"Go ahead—" Mami starts to say. That's all Coco needs to hear. She races out the door before Mami can finish her sentence. Unfortunately, I am not as quick as Coco.

"But make sure you bring a sweatshirt," Mami continues.

A sweatshirt. Of *course*.

"But it's still summer vacation," I protest, even though I know it doesn't matter. Mami *always* makes us take a sweatshirt when we go outside after dinner. Even if it's August.

"It never hurts to be prepared," she says.

Ordinarily I'd agree. But not today. "I can't wear my sweatshirt," I say. "It's *ruined*."

Mami turns to me and puts her hands on her hips. "Kitty-Cat, don't be so quisquillosa."

"Kee-skee-YO-sah," Papi repeats slowly. As if I haven't heard the word about a million times before.

"That means 'persnickety,'" he adds. "And 'persnickety' means 'picky.'" As if I didn't already know.

"Your sweatshirt is *not* ruined," Mami continues. "The pocket is torn, that's all. It is still perfectly wearable. Now, you'd better go get it before you waste any more daylight arguing with me."

I stomp upstairs. I am *not* quisquillosa. Or persnickety. And that sweatshirt is definitely *not* perfect.

Not like my books, I think as I gaze at the shelves on my side of the bedroom. They are organized by color and by author.

Coco doesn't organize her books. They don't even face the same direction. Some stand upright. Some lie on their sides.

Some are *missing their covers*.

"They don't give trophies for neatest bookshelf, you know," Coco said once when I tried to give her some helpful tips.

Well, maybe they should. Because maybe then I'd get one. Carlos might be the cutest, and Coco might be the most courageous. But I'm definitely the most perfectly put together in the family.

Not that anyone gives me any credit for it.

I open my closet. Everything is right where it belongs.

Except my gray sweatshirt.

Its hanger, right between my sundress and my swimsuit (I like to keep my clothes alphabetical too), is empty.

I check the floor—spotless, as usual.

I peek behind the shoe rack. The sweatshirt's not there either.

I take a deep breath. I hold my nose. I prepare to search inside Coco's closet. I am about to fling open the door when Tía Abuela calls out from the guest room, "Kitty-Cat? Is that you?"

I let out my breath. "Coming, Tía Abuela."

I find her sitting in the rocking chair by the window. My gray sweatshirt is folded on her lap. The velvet sewing pouch she gave me rests on the nightstand. I didn't even notice her taking it upstairs.

Tía Abuela might not be on television anymore, but she still sparkles. She always wears cat-eye sunglasses with crystals on the frames, even indoors. Her lips are cherry red, and she has silver hair that falls in gentle waves.

"It's time for a sewing lesson," she says. "Estás lista?"

Am I ready? Outside the window the sun is sinking fast. Already the clouds are pinky-orange. "Hmm. I was going to skate with Coco," I try to explain. "But then Mami said I needed—"

"Tu chamarra?" Tía Abuela pats my sweatshirt. "I saw it was torn and thought you might like to fix it. Almost finished. Ven acá."

I do what she says and come closer, then kneel on the rug at her feet.

Tía Abuela lifts her sunglasses to her forehead, and I yelp. "AAAH!"

It looks like two black spiders are crawling on Tía Abuela's eyelids!

Then I realize, my heart still pounding, that those aren't spiders. They're just her lashes. Impossibly long false eyelashes.

Tía Abuela bats her eyes. "How do you like them?" she asks. "They're new."

I catch my breath. I try to think of something polite to say. "They are . . . so . . . so . . . *different*."

Tía Abuela chuckles. She takes the needle and spool of thread from the velvet pouch. "Just one last stitch," she says.

She pulls a long gold chain up from inside her

zebra-print blouse. At the end of the chain is a tiny pair of gold scissors.

Tía Abuela uses them to snip a length of thread off the spool. She squints and pokes the thread through the needle's eye.

"I didn't know you could sew," I say.

She rolls her eyes. "Por favor! Of course I can sew, Kitty-Cat. I made all my own costumes when I was starting out, you know."

"Even the Dragon Dress?" I ask.

The Dragon Dress is one of La Chispa's most famous costumes and also my favorite. It is a long, shimmering gown covered in emerald beads, with fiery orange sunstones and blazing-red rubies around the neck. Tía Abuela has donated the dress to the Valle Grande library. It will be on display at the grand opening tomorrow.

"Even the Dragon Dress," Tía Abuela says

proudly. "Including all the gems—seventy-five of them, each stitched on by hand. It took me weeks to finish."

She hands me the needle and thread.

"But I've never sewn before," I protest, trying to give them back. "I don't know how."

Tía Abuela rocks forward and back. "Coser y cantar, todo es empezar."

"Huh?" I understand a lot of Spanish words, but sometimes I need help.

"From sewing to singing, it's all about starting," Tía Abuela translates. "It's an old saying that means 'Whatever it is you are trying to do, the most important thing is just to begin.'"

She shows me how to tie a knot at the end of the thread and where to draw the needle through the fabric to close the last raw edge of the torn pocket.

"Sewing is like magic," she says as we finish.

"Take a piece of cloth, a bit of thread, and with a few stitches and some imagination, you can turn it all into something new."

She holds up the sweatshirt. "See? Magia!"

That's when I realize she has done more than fix the pocket. Tía Abuela has made two kitten ears and sewn them onto the hood, and added a diamond-shaped patch between them.

A kitten. Of course.

"How do you like it?" she asks.

I fight back a frown. "Gracias, Tía Abuela. Only—"

"You're getting too old for kittens?" Tía Abuela pulls her sunglasses back down over her eyes. The crystals twinkle. "Try it on. You might be surprised."

· CHAPTER 3 ·

ʃHOO

*T*here isn't time to take the ears off the hood now, not if I want to skateboard before it gets dark. I dash down the stairs and tear the newspaper wrapping off Coco's old helmet.

Once outside, I listen for the *whiiirrrrrCRACK* of wheels rolling over pavement, leaping the curb, and landing with a clatter on the sidewalk. When I hear it, I follow the sound to the end of the block, where Coco and her friends stand with their skateboards.

Coco's turn is next. I watch her tighten the smelly old plaid flannel shirt she always wears tied around her waist. Mami has bought her lots of new shirts, but Coco insists that *this* one is lucky. It's the one she was wearing when she landed her first trick.

She steps onto her skateboard with one foot and pushes off with the other. With one more push, she sails across the street. Just when it looks like she is about to crash for sure, she steps down hard on the back of the deck. The skateboard jumps up and over the curb. Everyone cheers as she comes down again and glides to a stop.

I drop my sweatshirt onto the sidewalk.

I buckle the helmet strap under my chin. "I'm ready."

Coco turns around. "Ready to stay on the board, I hope." She kicks up her skateboard and catches it under her arm. "Unlike last time?"

"Very funny," I say. Even though it is very *not*.

It happened last summer at the skate park. Coco stood on her skateboard, teetering over the edge of what looked like an empty swimming pool. Then she crouched, leaned forward, and rolled down the smooth wall, up the other side, and back down again. Even I could admit it was pretty amazing.

When I asked for a turn, Coco told me I should practice on some of the smaller ramps first.

But Coco was always treating me like a baby. And, anyway, it had looked so easy when she'd done it.

"Have it your way," she said finally. "But don't blame me when you wipe out."

I stood with the skateboard hanging over the edge of the bowl. Just like Coco. I crouched down. I leaned forward. So far, so good . . . until the wheels slipped. I flung out my arms, trying to catch my balance. But it was too late. The skateboard rolled down the wall. And I went tumbling down behind it.

I haven't ridden a skateboard since then, but I have been watching Coco all summer. I have memorized every move. I will land the trick even more perfectly than she can. No mistakes.

I grab Coco's skateboard and set it on the ground in front of me.

"Fine, Cat," Coco says. "But you'd better borrow my kneepads too. I don't want to get in trouble when you go home full of bruises."

I am not going to go home full of bruises. I am going to go home a skating *star*. But I put the kneepads on anyway. I step on the board with one foot and push off with the other. Exactly like Coco. *Better* than Coco.

"Just take it slow at first, okay?" she says.

That only makes me push even harder. The skateboard speeds up. *I am doing it!* I think.

I fly faster and faster. The curb comes closer and closer.

Too close.

I jump off and stumble backward as the skate-board slams into the curb.

"Cat!" Coco yells, jogging over to check on her board.

Her friends laugh.

I yank off the helmet and Coco's pads, then run across the street for my sweatshirt. If only there hadn't been so many people watching, if only Coco didn't always treat me like a baby, I *know* I could have done it.

"Cat!" Coco calls after me again. I don't turn around. All I want to do is hide. So even though it isn't chilly outside—not even close—I put on my sweatshirt, zip it up to my chin, and pull the hood low over my forehead.

A chill runs down my back and straight to the tips of my fingers and toes. *Strange*, I think as I start walking again.

Mami is sweeping the front porch when I get home. She looks up when I start climbing the steps.

"Where do you think you're going? Shoo!" Mami says, waving the broom at me.

I dodge and try to go around her.

Mami steps in front of me. She blocks the door. She can't stand it when we track dirt inside, especially after she's just swept. But I *always* take my shoes off first. Unlike Coco.

"Oh, no you don't," Mami says. She backs into the house and slams the screen shut. "Shoo, Cat. Go away."

And she calls *me* persnickety.

I walk around to the side door that opens into the laundry room. I step out of my shoes, unzip my sweatshirt, and wriggle out of it.

In the kitchen Mami is emptying the dustpan into a wastebasket. Tía Abuela sits at the table with a book, *Useful Knots for the New Sailor*. In a few days she will leave Valle Grande to sail far away to the Galápagos Islands. Her sunglasses are pushed down to the very tip of her nose. She looks over them as she reads.

"Catalina," Mami says, "what have we told you

about feeding stray cats? When you feed them, they think they belong to us."

I don't know what she's talking about. "I haven't been feeding any strays," I say as I fill a glass with water.

"Oh, no? Then why did a cat just stroll up the front steps like she lived here?"

Now I'm even more confused. "I was outside a second ago," I say. "I didn't see any cats."

Tía Abuela glances up from her book. "What did the cat look like?"

"Gray," Mami says. "With a patch of white fur on her forehead. Like a diamond."

I almost spit out the water I gulped. That sounds almost exactly like—

Tía Abuela interrupts my thought. "Gray with a diamond-shaped patch of fur on her forehead?" she repeats. "You don't see that every day."

She looks at the sweatshirt draped over my arm, then straight into my eyes. She winks. Her spidery eyelashes flutter.

I swallow another drink of water.

Mami shakes her head. "No, I guess not. But the cat did look very familiar. I'm sure I've seen her before. . . . Anyway, the point is, I don't want you girls feeding animals. You're the only Kitty-Cat who's welcome around here, comprendes?"

I'm not sure I *do* understand, but I nod anyway.

Tía Abuela closes her book. "Kitty-Cat, I think you're ready for another sewing lesson."

CHAPTER 4

The Basics

*T*ía Abuela leads me to the guest room. She points to the edge of her bed, inviting me to sit.

But I can't sit. I can't even close my mouth.

"Don't look so sorprendida," Tía Abuela says. "Didn't I tell you sewing is like magic?"

"Surprised" is an understatement. "You didn't tell me it was *that* kind of magic. *Real* magic."

"Would you have believed me if I had?" she asks.

Probably not. In fact, I don't quite believe her

now. "You're saying the sewing kit . . . turned me into a cat?"

Tía Abuela clicks her tongue. "Por favor! Kitty-Cat, don't you think you would *know* if you had turned into a cat?"

I don't *feel* like a cat, but I look over my shoulder just in case. No tail. No fur.

Tía Abuela snorts.

"So, it just made Mami *think* I was a cat? Like a disguise?"

"Un disfraz. Sí, something like that," Tía Abuela agrees. "The person who wears the disguise must tie the last knot to seal the spell. Pero none of that matters if you don't know how to sew. The magic is only as strong as your stitches."

When I first unwrapped Tía Abuela's sewing kit, I didn't know what to do with it. Now ideas race through my mind so fast, I almost can't keep up with them.

I remember Coco's flannel shirts. Maybe I could turn one of them into a skater disfraz to trick Coco and her friends into taking me seriously.

"I know what to make!" I spring off the bed. "I'll be right back."

But Tía Abuela holds up a hand to stop me. Her gold bangles clink as they slide down her wrist. "Not so fast, señorita. First you need to learn the basics. Mi bolsa, por favor."

The basics? This is just like Coco making me start with the baby ramps at the skate park. I sigh and retrieve Tía Abuela's purse from the other side of the room. It is heavier than it looks.

She rummages through her bag, then pulls out a blue cookie tin. *Perfect*, I think. *I could use a snack.* Except instead of cookies inside, there are needles, thread, safety pins, and buttons.

"More sewing supplies?" I ask, trying not to

sound too disappointed. I guess *nothing* is what it appears to be.

"Sí. These ones are for everyday projects," she says. "Just what we need for practice. Primero, we thread the needle."

Tía Abuela holds up a needle, and the light from her reading lamp shines through its eye. She nods at me to make sure I'm paying attention. I nod back to show her I am.

Next she unspools some thread and snips it with her tiny gold scissors. She pinches one end of the thread between her thumb and pointer finger, squints, sticks out her tongue, and pokes the thread straight through the needle's eye.

Then she pulls the thread out again. "Now you try."

I pinch the thread between my thumb and finger. Just like Tía Abuela. I hold the needle up to the light and squint. I even stick out my tongue.

I aim . . . and miss.

I try again.

And then again.

My shoulders slump. "I'll never be any good at this." I let the needle and thread fall to my lap. Tía Abuela doesn't look up. She just sits in the  rocking chair, stitching on a scrap of fabric.

"Qué lástima," she says, shaking her head. "What a shame to waste all that magic."

I think about Coco's flannel and try again.

And again.

At last the thread slides through the needle's eye.

"Finally!"

"Sí, por fin," Tía Abuela repeats. "Now we can move on to the running stitch." She shows me the neat dashed line she has sewn along the edge of the fabric scrap, then hands it to me. "Your turn."

As Tía Abuela teaches me how to pull the thread—over, under, over, under—through the fabric, she tells me how she, too, received the red velvet sewing pouch on her eighth birthday.

"Pero, *I* did a better job of pretending to like it," she adds. "Of course, I was an actress, even then."

It was a gift from her mami, another Catalina, who had received it from *her* mami before that. "It's amazing how many problems you can solve with a needle and thread," she continues. "And not just rips and tears. My great-grandmother used hers to sew banners to rally for the right to vote. And her grandmother before that sewed a disguise to sneak into university classes when women were not allowed there. I wonder what you will create."

It sounds so important all of a sudden. "Why

did you give the sewing kit to *me*?" I ask. "Why not Papi?" I scowl. "Or . . . Coco?"

Tía Abuela pauses before answering. "I thought about that, but I needed someone more . . ." She taps her fingernail against her lips.

"Careful?" I suggest. "Orderly? Perfectly put together?"

Tía Abuela shakes her head. "Quisquillosa," she says. "And that's why it's your turn to keep the magic safe. We all start out with a fresh spool of thread, but remember, when your thread is gone, it's gone forever. So only use it when you really need it."

I finish my first row of stitches. Next to Tía Abuela's, they are crooked, uneven, loose. Not perfect. Not in order. Not even close.

"What a *mess*."

Tía Abuela leans over for a closer look. She lifts up her glasses. "Sí," she agrees.

I groan. "I wanted them to be perfect."

"Pues, they might never be *perfectos*," Tía Abuela says. "But they will be a little bit better each time you try."

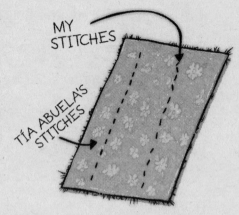

There is a gentle knock on the door. Papi peeks into the room. "Kitty-Cat?" he says. "Time to get some sleep. Tomorrow is a big day."

Tía Abuela winks at me. "Shoo, Kitty-Cat," she says. "I'll see you por la mañana."

But when I wake up the next morning, Tía Abuela isn't there.

CHAPTER 5

The Big Reveal

*T*ía Abuela doesn't answer when I knock on the guest room door. She isn't in the kitchen when I go downstairs to pour myself a bowl of cereal.

Only Papi is at the table, sipping his coffee and grading math exams from the summer school class he teaches at Valle Grande Community College.

"Where's Tía Abuela?"

"She walked down to the library already," he

says, glancing up from his work. "She wanted to get there early to make sure everything is ready for the grand opening."

I smile to myself. *Finally. Someone else who understands the importance of punctuality.* I only wish Tía Abuela had taken me with her.

After breakfast I go back upstairs to get dressed—and to plan my first sewing project.

Coco is still snoring softly on the top bunk. I reach up and poke her foot, then wait to see if she stirs. When she doesn't, I creep to her closet and snatch a plaid flannel shirt from the heap on the floor. Tía Abuela said to save the magic for when I really need it. After dreaming about skateboarding most of the night, I'm sure I *really* do.

Suddenly Coco rolls over and mumbles something. Sounds that aren't exactly words.

I stand perfectly still. I hold my breath.

When Coco starts snoring again, I hang her shirt up in my closet. She'll never even notice it's missing.

"We're going to be late," I warn my family for the eleventh time that day. I am pacing in front of the door, waiting to leave for the library.

"Kitty-Cat, you are being impatient," Papi says.

"And irritating," Coco grumbles.

By the time we finally walk down the hill to the library, a crowd has gathered inside the lobby. Standing front and center is a boy wearing a white guayabera and khaki pants. He holds an autograph book in one hand, a pen in the other.

I groan. "Pablo Blanco."

Pablo is my only real rival at Valle Grande Elementary. He's also sort of my friend. No one else in our class—or even our school—has our attention to detail.

Pablo's spelling is more precise. But my cursive is more impeccable.

I always stay late after school to make sure the whiteboards are wiped completely clean. Pablo arrives early to check that the clocks aren't running too fast or too slow.

I am La Chispa's grand-niece. He is La Chispa's number one fan.

But that doesn't mean he's allowed to touch the Dragon Dress.

The gown is in the middle of the lobby, hidden behind black curtains until the big reveal. As fans crowd into the room, Pablo inches closer and closer to the dress. He pulls back an edge of the curtain.

"Don't touch that!" I shout.

Pablo jumps. He looks at me and frowns.

"Catalina Castañeda," he says. He drops the curtain and buries one hand in his pocket. The other hand still clutches his autograph book and pen. He looks like he is about to argue, but then his eyes widen at something behind me.

I spin around. Josefina the Librarian and Tía Abuela have just stepped into the lobby. Tía Abuela wears a gold-studded jacket over black leather pants. The crystals on her sunglasses twinkle.

Pablo rushes toward her, holding out his pen and autograph book.

Tía Abuela laughs as she takes them from him.

"Por favor! Not another one, Pablo," she says. But she signs her name anyway.

She closes the book and hands it back.

"Una foto?" he asks.

Tía Abuela grins and tosses her silver waves. "Anything for my number one fan."

But before Pablo can take a picture, Josefina clears her throat. She looks down at her watch. Even from a distance I can tell it's the same one she always wears, silver with a cat's face on the front. The minute and hour hands look like whiskers. I used to wish I had one just like it. *Used* to, but not anymore.

"Oh," Tía Abuela says. "Is it time?" She strides to the center of the room, her high-heeled boots clacking against the floor tiles.

Josefina clears her throat again. Then, reading

from note cards, she tells the story of Tía Abuela's famous telenovela past.

"And now," Josefina the Librarian says, wrapping up, "it is my pleasure to dedicate the new Valle Grande Central Library children's room in honor of our generous patron, Catalina Castañeda."

Tía Abuela holds a hand over her heart. "Por favor, you can call me 'La Chispa.'"

Everyone cheers. Josefina the Librarian flips to another note card. "To mark the occasion," she goes on, "Catalina—La Chispa—has donated the 'Dragon Dress,' which she wore in . . ."

She shuffles the cards. "Which she wore in . . ."

Pablo stands on tiptoe. He raises his hand way up like when he's trying to answer a question in class.

"Which she wore in . . ."

"*A Heart of Fire!*" Pablo finally blurts.

"Yes, of course," Josefina the Librarian says.

"Which she wore in *A Heart of Fire*. Now, Catalina, will you do the honors?"

Tía Abuela whisks the curtains back and reveals the shimmering emerald gown.

Everyone cheers again.

"Magnífico!" Pablo sighs.

"A little much," Josefina mutters.

"It's *ruined!*" I yell.

A moment ago, everyone was staring at the Dragon Dress. Now they all whip their heads around to stare at me.

"Kitty-Cat?" Tía Abuela asks.

I push my way to the front. "Ruined," I say again. I point to the collar. I can't believe no one else has noticed the small empty space. "See? A ruby is missing. There."

Curious whispers buzz around the room.

"Missing? Por favor! Of course not," Tía Abuela

says. She laughs nervously and steps in front of the gown. "Everything is right where it belongs."

I check again, just to be sure.

And I'm *sure.* "No," I insist. "Look closer."

Visitors lean in. Some begin to point.

"It is a very old dress, Kitty-Cat," Tía Abuela says. "Maybe one of the stones just . . . popped off."

Impossible. I have seen Tía Abuela sew. Her

stitches are straight and strong. The ruby could *not* have just popped off.

I am about to say so when, out of the corner of my eye, I notice Pablo leaving the library.

"Hey, wait!" I call out. But he doesn't stop.

CHAPTER 6

Incognito

*T*ía Abuela stays at the library awhile longer to sign autographs. I can't stop thinking about the missing ruby as the rest of us walk home that afternoon.

"I wish I knew who had that missing ruby," I say.

No one answers. We walk past four more houses. "I wonder if we will *ever* find that missing ruby."

"Kitty-Cat, this is getting tedious," Mami complains.

"And tiresome," adds Papi. "If Tía Abuela isn't

worried about it, you shouldn't be either. Try to let it go."

But I can't. Someone has ruined Tía Abuela's most famous costume. Now the only thing I'll ever see when I look at the Dragon Dress is the empty space where a ruby should sparkle. It's like a puzzle with a piece missing, which is the worst thing that can happen to a puzzle. Even worse than baby slobber.

No matter what she says, Tía Abuela must be upset about what's happened. I have to get that ruby back before she leaves.

And I know just where to start looking.

I burst through the front door as soon as Mami opens it. I don't take off my shoes first. I don't even stomp the dust off. I run upstairs and open my closet. I shove aside Coco's flannel—the disfraz will have to wait—and grab my gray sweatshirt. *That* gray sweatshirt.

"I'm going to visit Pablo," I say as I scramble back down the stairs.

"Sure thing, Kitty-Cat," Mami says. "But don't forget to take a—"

"Sweatshirt," I say as I'm stepping out the door. "I know."

Halfway down the block, I hide behind a trash bin. When I am sure no one is looking, I slip my arms into the sweatshirt and zip it up to my chin. I pull the hood over my head and feel a shiver flutter down my spine. That must mean I am incognito. Disguised, I scurry to Pablo's house.

It's easy to tell which window is his. It's the cleanest. No spots, no streaks. I borrow a basketball from the neighbor's yard and carefully climb on top of it to peek inside Pablo's room.

I'm so startled when I see my reflection in the window that I nearly tumble off the ball. Staring back at me is a gray cat with sleek fur and long, silky whiskers. *Purrr-fectly put together*, I think.

But I can't just stand here admiring myself. I look past my reflection and into the room. No one is inside. The first thing I notice is Pablo's bookshelf. He has organized his books, not just by color but also by . . . height?

I shake my head. *Focus*, I remind myself.

I press my nose against the window. Framed photographs, some of Tía Abuela and some of other actors, are arranged on top of Pablo's desk. Autographed posters hang on the walls. An enormous silver belt buckle gleams from inside its own display case. The buckle must have been a prop on one of those telenovelas set on an old rancho.

But I don't see the ruby. Not even a twinkle of it.

Pablo's door opens, and I dip my head. When I poke it up again, Pablo is standing at his desk. He reaches into his pocket for something. Could it be the gem?

Before I can get a closer look, the basketball rolls under my feet. I grasp at the windowsill, trying to steady myself, but the ball spins away. "AAH!" I scream, but it comes out like a kitten's yowl. I land on the ground, hard enough to shake the hood off my head.

The window opens.

Pablo sticks his head out. He looks left. He looks right.

He looks down.

"Oh," he says. "It's just you. Catalina Castañeda." He glances left and right again. "I thought I saw a cat out here. I'm allergic. *And* I didn't want its dirty paws on my windows. I just cleaned them this morning."

I stand and dust off my leggings. "Really? This morning? You know, you left some streaks."

Pablo scowls. "You know, there's dirt all over your nose."

I turn away from him and swipe my face with my sleeve. Then I narrow my eyes. "You sure left the library in a hurry. It didn't have anything to do with the missing ruby, did it?"

Pablo leans out the window. "Of course it did."

*H*as Pablo actually confessed?

"Give it back, then," I demand.

Pablo crosses his arms over his chest. "Give what back?"

"The ruby from the Dragon Dress, of course," I tell him. "You just admitted you took it."

"*Me?*" He gasps. "Damage one of the most important costumes in telenovela history? Nunca." *Never.* He shudders. "But I think I know who did. I came straight home to be sure. Hold on a minute."

Pablo ducks back into his room and returns with a black scrapbook. He hands it down to me. "Don't you see? This is *just* like what happened in the telenovela *My Sister, the Stranger.* I've been trying to explain it to my mom, but she thinks it's just a coincidence."

I flip through the scrapbook. Each page is filled with pictures and articles cut out of old magazines. I don't understand what Pablo is talking about. "You're not trying to distract me, are you?" I ask. "Throw me off the trail?"

Pablo shakes his head. "Move over," he says. "I'll explain."

I step back as Pablo swings his legs out the window and hops down. He lands on his feet. Just like a cat.

Of *course.*

Pablo snatches back the scrapbook and opens it to a page near the end.

"Here," he says, holding the page open for me to see. He points to a black-and-white picture of Tía Abuela taken when she was about Papi's age. She looks dangerous, with arching eyebrows and snarling lips.

There's another picture right next to it. It's of Tía Abuela too, only I don't recognize her at first. She looks friendlier in this one, with a sunny smile and a dimple in each cheek.

I start to read the caption aloud. "Paulina Mendez has it all: a perfect house, a perfect job, a perfect family—"

Pablo closes his eyes and recites the rest of the words by heart:

DOUBLE TROUBLE

"Until a stranger comes to town—Paulina's long-lost twin, who is determined to steal everything Paulina loves."

He opens his eyes and looks at me as if that explains everything.

It does not.

"So Tía Abuela was playing twin sisters," I say. "What does that have to do with the missing ruby?"

"Ugh." Pablo flips to another page. "Here."

It is Tía Abuela again, only much younger. In this picture she is laughing, her arm around another girl's shoulders.

"I feel like I've seen that girl before," I say. "But I don't know where."

Pablo rolls his eyes. "Just *read*."

"Catalina Castañeda and Josefina Chavez star as mischievous twins in *Double Trouble*."

Pablo taps the picture of Josefina with his finger.

"*Now* do you understand? Josefina the Librarian starred in a telenovela too—with La Chispa. But that was Josefina's first and only role. She could never be a star. She must have gotten jealous over the years. So jealous that she decided to ruin La Chispa's big moment *and* her most famous costume."

I roll up my sweatshirt sleeves and lean against the side of Pablo's house to think. I try to remember everything that happened at the library this afternoon.

"I guess Josefina did seem a little impatient," I say.

Still, I am not convinced that Pablo hasn't stolen the ruby himself. Finding out Josefina has it would be one way to know for sure.

"I'm going back to the library to check it out," I say. "And you're coming with me." I can't risk letting him out of my sight.

"Of course I am," Pablo says. He stands on tiptoe

to drop the scrapbook back through his bedroom window. "*You* wouldn't know how to take care of the ruby if you found it."

We both look down at our watches. "Too late," we say at the same time.

"It's 5:01," Pablo says.

"It's 5:01 and thirty-seven seconds," I correct him. "The library closed at five. But it opens again tomorrow at ten a.m. Don't be late."

CHAPTER 8

BETTER THAN BEFORE

Walking back home, I hear the roll and smack of Coco's skateboard on the sidewalk.

Then I hear new sounds: *Thud.* "Uf! Ow!"

I run ahead and find Coco sitting on the curb. She is rubbing her shoulder.

"Are you okay?"

Coco looks up. "You didn't just see that."

"No," I say. "I heard it, though."

Coco pushes the skateboard toward me. It rolls to my feet. "You should try again," she says.

I push it back to her with the toe of my sneaker. She just wants to see me *fall* again. "No way."

Coco wipes her palms on her flannel shirt, still tied around her waist. Then she holds out her arms like Baby Carlos does when he wants to be carried.

"Fine. Help me up."

I grab Coco's hands and pull. "What happened? You never fall."

"I fall all the time when I'm learning a new trick," she admits. She tightens the helmet strap under her chin. "But this time I'm going to land it. I can feel it."

I can't believe what I'm hearing. "You're not actually going to do that again, are you?" I ask. "Aren't you scared you'll mess up?"

Coco shrugs. "If I'm afraid to mess up, I'll lose my chance to get better." She hops back onto her skateboard.

I step out of her way.

Coco pushes down with her back foot and jumps up with the other as the board spirals underneath her.

For a split second she hangs in the air, and I think, *She's doing it!*

But when Coco comes back down, the board skids out from under her, and she thumps to the sidewalk again. I cringe. I expect her to scream. Instead she smiles. "That was my best one yet!" Then she holds out her arms again. "Help."

I pull Coco to her feet and glance down at the skateboard. If she can get that excited about falling, it might be worth another try after all.

"Maybe . . ." But no. I can't do it. "Never mind."

"Why not?" Coco unbuckles her helmet and lifts

it off. "Don't tell anyone I said this, but you didn't do that bad the other day."

"I didn't?"

She shakes her head. "No. You were way better than that time at the skate park. I bet you stayed on the board a whole five seconds. Think you can make it to six?" She tosses the helmet to me.

I catch it but don't put it on. "Some other time," I reply. Standing on a skateboard for six seconds doesn't seem like much, especially compared to what Coco can do. "After I've watched you some more. Then I'll be ready."

I try to give the helmet back, but Coco pushes it toward me again.

"Come on, Cat. You won't start to get better until you . . . *start*."

It reminds me of what Tía Abuela said about sewing. About how, whether it's sewing or singing—

or skateboarding—the most important thing is to begin.

"Well . . ." I look around. It's only me and my sister. No one else is watching. "Maybe just one more time."

Coco pumps her fist. "Yes!" She picks up the skateboard and positions it in front of me. "Now, bend your knees a little. That will help you balance."

I step on top of the board. It wobbles underneath my feet, and I fling my arms out to steady myself. "Whoa."

"Bend," Coco reminds me.

I nod and bend my knees. She's right! I don't feel like I'm about to topple over anymore. I pick up my back leg and get ready to give myself a giant push.

"Wait!" Coco yells.

"Wait?" I thought she wanted me to start. I put my foot on the ground and look up at her.

"Take it slow."

This time I listen. I push gently off my back foot, and the skateboard rolls forward. With me still on top of it.

Coco starts counting. "One! Two! Three!"

I'm not slipping. I'm not stumbling. I'm staying on! I count along with her. "Four! Five!"

When we get to six, I jump off the board and spin around. Coco is already running toward me. "You did it!" She raises her hand for a high five.

I might not be better than Coco. But I'm definitely better than before. I slap her hand, and we walk the rest of the way home together.

CHAPTER 9

ACCIDENTS HAPPEN

Onions sizzle in a frying pan, and steam curls over a pot. "Dinner will be ready in half an hour," Papi says as Coco and I step into the kitchen. "Why don't you two wash up?"

Baby Carlos sits on the floor, surrounded by pots and pans. He smacks a wooden spoon against a metal mixing bowl. *Clang, clang, clang.*

I kneel down to ruffle his feathery brown hair.

He gurgles, then grabs one of the kitten ears on

my sweatshirt. He clutches it in his fist and pulls it toward his mouth.

"No, no, Carlos." I shake the sweatshirt gently, trying to loosen it from his hands.

But Carlos won't let go. His grip only tightens.

I pick up a set of measuring spoons and jangle them in front of his nose. Carlos bats the spoons away. He tugs on my hood again, this time with both hands.

I tug too until . . . *Rrrrriiip.*

"Uh-oh," Carlos says. He lets go of the ear and lets it drop to the floor.

"Carlos, no! My sweatshirt! It's—" I am about to say "ruined." Papi stops stirring the onions and waits for me to finish.

"It's . . . something I can fix," I say instead.

"Bravo," Papi says. "Good attitude, Kitty-Cat. Accidents happen." He goes back to stirring the onions. Carlos goes back to drumming on the mixing bowl.

It might be true that accidents happen, but this one could not have happened at a worse time. If I'm going to investigate Josefina the Librarian, I'm going to need to sneak into her office. And if I'm going to sneak into her office, I'm going to need a disfraz. A good one.

I take the sweatshirt, the loose kitten ear, and the red velvet sewing pouch to Tía Abuela's room.

She is reading again—a book called *Fashion for*

the High Seas. I hate to interrupt her, but this is urgent. "Can we have another sewing lesson?" I hold the sweatshirt in one hand and the scrap of fabric that used to be a kitten ear in the other.

Tía Abuela closes her book and sets it on the nightstand.

"Qué pasó, Kitty-Cat?" she asks.

"Carlos happened." I flop down onto the bed.

Tía Abuela sits next to me. "Well, go on, then," she says. "Let's see if you remember how to thread a needle."

I open the pouch and pull the needle from the strawberry pincushion. I unwind a little of the silvery thread and tear it between my teeth. I aim. I squint. And . . . I miss.

But this time I don't get discouraged. I imagine Coco stepping back onto her skateboard even after she falls. I try again, slow and steady, and the thread slips through the needle's eye.

"Bravo! You're getting better already." Tía Abuela pats my shoulder.

"I think I am!" I agree. But knowing how long it will take to get as good as she is makes me even more upset about the Dragon Dress.

"Doesn't it bother you that someone stole the ruby and spoiled all your hard work?"

Tía Abuela twirls one of the gold bangles around her wrist. "How do you know it was stolen?"

I think about Pablo and how much he'd probably love to add a piece of the Dragon Dress to his collection.

I think about Josefina and how badly she might have wanted to steal Tía Abuela's spotlight.

But I don't have any proof. Yet.

"You don't *really* think it just popped off on its own, do you?"

"Hmm," Tía Abuela replies. Not quite a yes, but not exactly a no. She changes the subject. "Are you going to fix that sweatshirt, or what?" She holds the kitten ear against the sweatshirt hood. "Unless . . ."

She pauses and pulls out her tiny gold scissors. "Didn't you say you were getting too old for kittens? Maybe you would rather snip both ears off instead?"

"No! I *need* . . . I mean, I *want* the ears. You were right. The sweatshirt was missing something." I wink—just like Tía Abuela does—and we get to work.

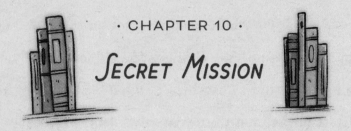

· CHAPTER 10 ·

Secret Mission

The next morning I get to the library at exactly 9:55 and forty-six seconds. My sweatshirt, with both ears sewn on, is tucked under my arm.

Pablo is already waiting at the entrance. He taps his toe against the pavement. When he sees me, he looks down at his watch. "You're almost late," he says. Behind me Mami is towing Baby Carlos down the hill in a red wagon. Coco rolls alongside them on her skateboard. "And you brought company. I thought this was a *secret* mission."

"Couldn't help it."

When I asked Mami if I could walk down to the library this morning, she insisted on coming along. "Carlos loves Baby Story Time," she said. "And my shift at the nursing home doesn't start until this afternoon." Plus, it's Coco's day to volunteer with the summer reading club, so Mami thought we should all walk together.

She parks the wagon. "See, Kitty-Cat, I told you it was too early," she says. "The library isn't even open yet."

Pablo steps toward her. "You know what they say, Señora Castañeda, 'El que madruga coge la oruga.' The early bird catches the worm."

Then he leans toward me and whispers, "But *we're* here to catch a jewel thief."

"Shh," I hiss. By now there are almost a dozen

people waiting for the library to open. "Someone will hear you."

Finally Josefina the Librarian unlocks the doors. Visitors step aside to let Mami roll the wagon in. Carlos gurgles and claps. Coco leaves her skateboard just inside the entrance.

Pablo and I let everyone else file past us.

"So, what's our plan?" he asks, his voice low.

I figured it all out last night. "Here's what we're going to do: I'll ask Josefina if I can help her shelve books. She'll go get the cart. That's your signal. When she comes back, get her to follow you to the history section. It's usually pretty empty there. And then *I'll* sneak into her office to look for the ruby."

"But what about the 'Staff Only' doors?" he asks. "They're always locked."

"Just leave it to me," I say.

Pablo's eyes flash. "This is *exactly* like what happened in the final episode of *Casa Misteriosa*." Then he notices my sweatshirt. "You know it's August, right? You're not *cold*, are you?"

I raise one eyebrow. "It's like my tía abuela says, 'You might be surprised.'"

We go inside. Josefina and her assistant, Ernest, are arranging cushions around a rainbow-colored rug for Baby Story Time. Mami sits down, but she has to get right back up when Carlos crawls away toward a shelf of alphabet books.

I lean against a magazine rack and look around.

A few steps away, a boy plunks three books down onto the reference desk, and Coco stamps his summer reading passport.

Some older kids sit at a study table, flipping through comics. Nearby, people sit down at the computer stations. The keyboards *click, click, click* as they type.

In the middle of it all, the Dragon Dress is on display behind velvet ropes. My eyes zoom to the ugly empty space where that ruby should sparkle.

I reach for a magazine. *Kittens Today*.

Of course.

I turn the pages, pretending to read them, until I see Josefina walking toward me.

"I see you found our newest subscription," she says. "I ordered it just for you. We cat lovers need to look out for each other."

Quickly I put the magazine back on the rack. "Gracias," I say, "but I don't really . . ." I am about to say I don't really like all that cat stuff anymore. But there isn't time to waste. I have a mission.

"Yes?" Josefina asks.

"I mean, I don't really . . . want to look at magazines right now. Do you have any books I can help put away?"

Josefina smiles. "Wait here. I'll go get the cart."

I knew she wouldn't suspect a thing. Shelving books—putting them back *exactly* where they belong—is pretty much my favorite thing to do at the library.

Pablo peers out from behind the biographies. I nod at him.

"Here you go, Catalina," Josefina says when she returns with the cart. "Why don't you start with—"

Right on time as always, Pablo interrupts us. "Señora Josefina!" he shouts, coming up behind her. "I have been looking all over for you."

Josefina jumps. She clutches the cat-shaped turquoise pendant she always wears. "Pablo Blanco," she says. "What have I told you about sneaking up on people like that? I'll be with you in a moment. I am just—"

He doesn't let her finish.

"But this is *important*," Pablo insists. "My mom and I just started watching *Doña Laura, the Scholar* last night, and now I need to find out everything there is to know about the National University of San Marcos. It's a real place, you know. In Peru."

Josefina the Librarian looks from Pablo to me and

back to Pablo. "Yes, I know it's a real place, Pablo," she says. "We can start in the South American history section if you'll wait just a—"

"South American history?" Pablo says. "Vamos!" *Let's go.* He takes Josefina's wrist and leads her to the other side of the library.

"Don't worry, Señora Josefina." I wave. "I know what to do."

As they disappear behind the shelves, I make sure the coast is clear. Baby Story Time has just started. Mami and Carlos clap along as Ernest strums a guitar. The boy with the reading passport is searching for new books. The older kids are still reading their comics.

With everyone distracted, I wheel the cart down the hallway and crouch behind it.

I unfold my sweatshirt and remember Tía Abuela's warning. *The magic is only as strong as your stitches.* My stitches are still not as straight as Tía Abuela's. But I hope they're strong enough.

I push my arms through the sleeves and zip the sweatshirt up to my chin. A chill runs down my back as I pull the hood over my head. I am incognito.

CHAPTER 11

CLUES

Using the library cart as a shield, I creep toward the history section. I don't want anyone to see me before Josefina does.

Just as I predicted, she and Pablo are the only ones here. "You might also be interested in Peruvian music," Josefina is saying as she adds another book to the stack in Pablo's arms. "And maybe food."

This is my chance. I slip out from behind the cart.

Pablo sees me first. His nose begins to twitch. "Cat?"

I freeze, worried he has recognized me. But then Pablo drops all the books he's holding right in time to cover a gigantic sneeze.

Achoo!

"Salud," Josefina says, stretching to pull a book off the top shelf. "Did you say 'cats'? Animal books are in a completely different section, Pablo."

"NO!" he says, pointing. "Cat!" *Achoo!* "Right there! I can't even"—*Achoo!*—"look at them without sneezing."

He races to the other side of the library.

Josefina bends down. "Well, hello there," she says. "How did you get in?"

She reaches out to pat my head, and I skitter away. I'm not *really* a cat, after all, and I don't know what might happen if she touches me.

"You're shy," Josefina says. "That's all 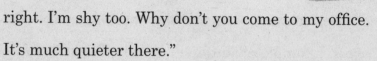 right. I'm shy too. Why don't you come to my office. It's much quieter there."

"Perfecto!" I shout. Only, it comes out like a purr. I trot behind Josefina as she leads the way across the library and down the hall. She waves a badge at the STAFF ONLY doors to unlock them, and we step right through.

I follow Josefina to her office, and she switches on the lights. "Make yourself at home," she says before leaving. "You'll be safe in here."

As soon as the door shuts behind her, I go

straight for the desk, searching for the gleam of a bright, red ruby. Instead the glint of a silver picture frame catches my eye. Inside there's a black-and-white photo like the one I saw in Pablo's scrapbook, of Tía Abuela and Josefina when they were young.

Engraved along the bottom edge of the frame are the words "Amigas para siempre."

"Friends forever," I say to myself.

This doesn't seem like the kind of thing Josefina would keep on her desk if she were jealous. In fact, it makes me think she might really *like* Tía Abuela.

And she must really *love* being a librarian, I realize. Taped above Josefina's desk are dozens of handwritten notes. *Thank you for the library tour! Thank you for helping me find the perfect book! Thank you for reading to our class!* There are drawings too, some in crayon, some in marker. Even in the drawings that are really scribbly, I can still make out Josefina's long gray hair and her cat-shaped pendant.

Pablo Blanco was wrong. Josefina didn't want to steal the spotlight. It shines on her right here in the library.

I am about to sneak back out to tell him this, when I hear Josefina's footsteps. I jump away from her desk as she's opening the door.

"It's lucky I always keep one of these in my car in case I come across a stray on my drive home." She's holding a pet carrier! "Let's get you inside so you'll be all ready to go when our friends from the animal rescue get here."

I can't let Josefina trap me in the carrier. For one thing, I won't fit! For another, I'll be caught! I bolt.

"Stop!" Josefina yells. "I wish I could let you stay here, but I can't."

I race through the STAFF ONLY doors—which, fortunately, Josefina propped open—to the circulation desk and jump behind it. I try to yank off the sweatshirt hood, but it snags on my barrette.

It isn't long before Josefina catches up. "There you are!" She waves a piece of cheese at me. "Here, Kitty-Cat," she says. "It's Swiss, from my lunch. I'll share it with you if you'll just climb into this cozy carrier."

I have to get out of the sweatshirt. But not where Josefina—or anyone else—can see.

I scurry around the desk, then jump over the study table.

I zigzag around the computer stations.

I dart past the boy looking for summer reading books, knocking over the stack he has piled up.

I scramble through the center of the story time circle. Babies wiggle out of their parents' laps and crawl after me. Carlos leads the pack. "Kitty!" he yells.

Things couldn't possibly get any worse. Babies are chasing me from one direction, Josefina from the other.

I back up until I bump against the dress stand. I am cornered.

I have no choice. I'm about to unzip the sweatshirt—about to reveal the secret of the magic sewing kit.

But then Josefina the Librarian shrieks.

"A spider!"

She kicks at something black and crawly. The thing shoots up into the air, then lands on my head. I pluck it off. Josefina was wrong. It isn't a spider, but I'm just as surprised by it as she is.

Josefina backs away, giving me one last chance to make an escape.

Coco's skateboard is still standing just inside the library entrance. If I can get to it, I might be able to roll away fast enough that Josefina can't catch me— if I don't fall off, that is.

I take a deep breath and race for the skateboard. I pull it away from the wall and jump on. Then, just as the animal rescue volunteer opens the library's front door, I push off with my foot and sail right past him.

I count in my head.

One! Two! Three!

I'm doing it! I'm skateboarding!

Four! Five! Six!

Not until I get to seven do I notice the planter box coming closer and closer.

Too close.

I crash and tumble into an azalea bush.

$\mathcal{L}$OST

I walk back into the library, out of breath. My sweat-shirt is crumpled under my arm.

Pablo rushes toward me. "Where have you been? You will never believe what you just missed—it was like a scene straight out of *Curse of the Panther.*"

He stops and frowns. "What happened to your hair?"

I touch my head. Curls spring out from my temples. I pull an azalea blossom out from behind my ear.

"And your shirt?" he asks. "You're really a mess, you know."

I look down. My shirt is rumpled and half-untucked. I'm not even close to perfectly put together. For once, though, I don't mind.

Pablo smooths his hand over his crisp, white guayabera as if checking to make sure *his* clothes are still in order. He lowers his voice, "So, did you find the ruby in Josefina's office?"

I pat my pocket. "No," I say. "She doesn't have it. But I think I know who does." Not Josefina. Not Pablo.

"Wait, but—" Pablo scratches his head.

"I'll explain everything later," I whisper as Mami walks toward us, pulling the wagon with Baby Carlos asleep inside.

"All that excitement seems to have tired your brother out," Mami says. "Ready to go home, Kitty-Cat?"

"I'm ready."

Outside we wave goodbye to Josefina and the animal rescue volunteer, who are poking around the azalea bushes, looking for a lost cat they'll never find. At least I hope they won't.

Just to be safe, I clutch the sweatshirt even tighter.

"Did you get a look at that cat?" Mami asks as we trudge up the hill. "I'm almost certain it was the same one that was hanging around our front porch the other day."

"Hmm," I reply. Not quite a yes, and not exactly a no.

· CHAPTER 13 ·

THE START

Tía Abuela sits in the rocking chair, sewing. Light from the reading lamp winks off her needle.

"What are you working on?" I ask.

She holds up a white blouse with a square sailor collar.

"Tía Abuela! That's not a magic shirt, is it? Un disfraz?"

She raises an eyebrow above her dark glasses.

I lower my voice. "You're not going to trick people

into believing you're a real sailor, are you?"

Tía Abuela throws back her head and laughs. Her sunglasses nearly slip off, but she catches them with her fingertips. "Por favor! Of course not, Kitty-Cat."

I kneel on the carpet in front of her. With my fingertip I trace the neat line of stitches she has already sewn on the shirt.

"Missing something," I say finally.

Tía Abuela tilts her head. "The shirt? I know it's a little plain, Kitty-Cat, but I can't exactly wear an evening gown at sea."

I shake my head. "No, *you're* missing something."

I reach into my pocket and pull out a fake eyelash. The one Josefina mistook for a spider. I drop it onto the nightstand.

Tía Abuela lifts her sunglasses to the top of her head. Just as I suspected, one of her eyelids is bare.

"Ah," Tía Abuela says. "I wondered where that went."

"It was in the library," I explain. "Underneath the Dragon Dress. That's how I knew *you* were the one who took the ruby. But I still don't know *why*."

Tía Abuela sighs. "I've never sailed before, and I was beginning to get nervous," she confesses. "I wanted something to remind me that, at one time, I had never sewn before. But I learned how, stitch by stitch. And the only way to finish a masterpiece like the Dragon Dress . . ."

I complete the sentence for her. ". . . is to start."

"Así es," Tía Abuela agrees. *That's right.* Slowly

she lifts an edge of the sailor collar. The ruby sparkles underneath.

She explains how, knowing Josefina would keep her secret, she went to the library early to take a jewel from the Dragon Dress. That must have been when she lost the eyelash. "I didn't think anyone would notice," she says. "I should have known *you* would."

Downstairs the front door opens. Seconds later Tía Abuela and I hear the *rrrrrrrooooollllSMACK* of Coco's skateboard on the sidewalk.

My head snaps up.

"Ándale," Tía Abuela says, picking up her sewing again.

I hesitate. I want to go. Only, I know it will be a long time before I can take another sewing lesson from Tía Abuela.

"But you're leaving tomorrow," I say. "And I still need practice."

"A *lot* of practice." Tía Abuela nods.

Then she winks. "Mi amiga Josefina can help. She's starting a new Stitch and Share group at the library. She'll be expecting you at the first meeting. Don't be late."

As if I am *ever* late.

I stop at my bedroom before heading outside. I already have my sweatshirt, but there's something else I need: Coco's flannel.

Not for un disfraz. I'll become a skater for real. With practice. Even if it means I have to mess up a lot more.

Instead I toss the shirt back into my sister's closet. Right where it belongs. Then I grab my helmet and race outside to try again.

Acknowledgments

It was my grandmother Mary Espinoza who taught me to sew. Without her patient and steady hands, this story would not be possible. I am forever grateful to her and to my Nana Josephine, to whom this book is dedicated, for showing me the many forms, some quieter than others, that creativity can take.

Mil gracias to my agent, Jennifer Laughran, who saw what this book could be, and to Alyson Heller, whose love for the family story at the heart of *Catalina Incognito* shone through in her wise and brilliant editing. I feel incredibly lucky to have worked with illustrator Gladys José, who brought Catalina to life with such charm and, yes, attention to detail! And with designer Laura DiSiena, Elizabeth Mims, Olivia Ritchie, Amelia Jenkins, Valerie Garfield, Kristin Gilson, and everyone else on the Aladdin team.

Finally, thank you to David, Alice, and Soledad. You inspire me all the time.

Turn the page for a
sneak peek at Catalina's
next magical adventure!

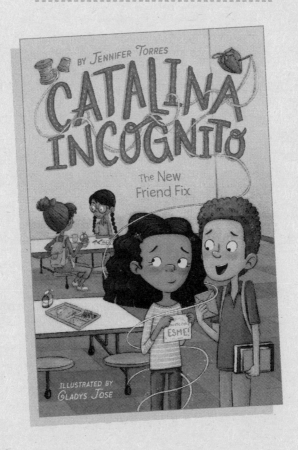

First Day

I have already slurped the last sugary drops of cereal milk off my spoon by the time my big sister, Coco, stumbles to the table.

She yawns and rubs her eyes, then asks, "You're already dressed, Cat?"

"Of course I am." It's the first day of school, after all. Last night I spent two hours organizing my backpack, filling the pouches and pockets with freshly sharpened pencils, never-used erasers, and notebooks with nothing but blank pages inside. Everything is perfectly put together.

Stuffing a backpack with new school supplies is one of my all-time favorite activities. Which means the day before school starts is one of my all-time favorite days of the year.

"But it's so early," Coco whines.

"It's never too early to be prepared," I answer.

Papi sets a bowl of cereal in front of Coco while I carry my empty bowl to the sink.

"Buenos días!" he greets her.

"Ugh," Coco moans.

Baby Carlos, our little brother, bangs his palms against his high chair tray, and Papi drops a few chunks of strawberry onto it. Carlos picks one up and mashes it in his fist.

Even though his sticky hands can't reach me, I still take a big step backward. Just in case.

Mami walks into the kitchen dressed in purple scrubs, all set for her shift at the nursing home.

"Are you excited to start middle school?" she asks, ruffling Coco's sleep-tangled hair.

Coco shrugs.

No one asks if I'm excited to start third grade. Maybe they think it will be just like any other year. Unlike Coco, I'm not going to a new school. But there will still be a new classroom, a new teacher, and—according to my best friend, and biggest rival, Pablo Blanco—a new kid. He heard all about her because his mom is the room parent.

Just one more reason to get to school early. Then *I'll* get to meet the new girl before anyone else does. Even Pablo.

I check to make sure my double-knotted shoelaces haven't come undone, then swing my backpack over my shoulder.

"See you later!" I announce.

Carlos gurgles and waves his gooey hand. Mami and Papi walk over to hug me goodbye.

"Have a wonderful day, mija," Papi says.

"I can't wait to hear all about it," Mami adds, and kisses my forehead.

"Wait!" Coco's mouth is full of frosted wheat squares. "What's the hurry? Give me a few more minutes, and I'll walk with you. Like always."

My hand hovers over the doorknob. Coco and I used to walk to school together every day. But I never thought she actually *wanted* to.

"But we don't go to the same school anymore, remember?" I say, turning the knob.

"We can walk to the corner at least," Coco persists. "I'll even let you ride my skateboard."

Hmm. Coco has been teaching me to ride her skateboard all summer. But only in front of our house. She's never offered to let me ride it anywhere else before.

Even Mami and Papi are surprised.

"Did you hear that, Kitty-Cat?" Papi asks. "Coco says you can ride her skateboard!"

I am tempted to tell Coco yes.

I am tempted to tell Papi to quit calling me "Kitty-Cat."

But, *no*, I decide. There isn't time. I need to get to school. I only have one chance to be the first person to meet the new girl. Then I'll get to introduce her to everyone else. Maybe our teacher will even pick me to show her around school.

"Thanks anyway, Coco," I say. "Maybe tomorrow."

I am stepping out the door when Coco stops me *again*.

"You're wearing *that*?"

My shoulders drop. I hoped no one would notice.

"Didn't you say you were getting too old for all the kitten stuff?" Coco continues.

Slowly I turn around. Coco is pointing at the gray sweatshirt tied around my waist. Two kitten ears and a diamond-shaped patch of white fur are sewn to the hood.

"At least I don't sleep in it too," I say, pointing back at the old flannel shirt Coco *never* takes off.

Coco straightens the collar. "This shirt is *lucky*."

"Well, this sweatshirt," I answer, "is . . . *special*."

"That's right," Mami says. She wraps her arm around my shoulders and squeezes. "Tía Abuela sewed the ears on herself. And I'm sure Kitty-Cat likes wearing it because she misses Tía Abuela. Isn't that right?"

I nod. Tía Abuela is my great-aunt. Her name is Catalina Castañeda just like mine. She used to be a famous telenovela actress. Ever since she retired,

Tía Abuela spends most of her time traveling the world. She doesn't come to our house on the hill in Valle Grande very often, so I *do* miss her.

But that's not the only reason why this sweatshirt is special.

On her last visit Tía Abuela gave me a musty old sewing kit in a red velvet pouch. Inside is a needle and spool of silvery thread. They don't sew regular clothes, though. They create magical disguises. Like this sweatshirt. As soon as I zip it up and pull on the hood, I'll look exactly like an *actual* cat. Over the summer I even used my disfraz to solve a major mystery. So far I haven't shared the secret of the sewing kit with *anyone*.

Before she left on her latest adventure, Tía Abuela warned me that the magic would only be as strong as my stitches. Since I'm still learning, I haven't been able to sew a new disfraz yet. That's why I'm stuck with this one. Even if I *am* getting too old for all this kitten stuff.

I look down at my watch. "Better go," I say. "You know how I feel about being late."

Mami and Papi shudder. Even Coco stops arguing.

I smile to myself and scamper down the front porch steps and out to the sidewalk. Once I'm a few houses down, where I'm sure my family can't see me, I duck behind a mailbox.

I look left and right to make sure no one is watching. I put on the sweatshirt and zip it to my chin. Then I lift the hood over my head. A chill runs up my spine.

I stand and glance down at my shadow on the pavement. It's not the shadow of a girl anymore. It's the shadow of a cat.

I am *incognito*.

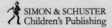

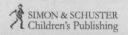